Prompted and Circumstanced

(A Fantastical Collection of Short Stories)

By: Michael "Fynn" Lange

Table of Contents

To Rod,
My photographer, my apartment sharer, my celebrator of little
and big accomplishments, and in total my other half.
You put up with all these stories and read them because you
knew if I kept them inside I would explode.

Sharer's of my works,
"Picture of a Man Who Couldn't" and "The Trail of Two
Brothers" have been featured in PicN'Story, A Creative
Global Webzine (www.picnstory.com)

The Sweetly Twisted Tale of Misses Sweet
(The Lie of Hansel & Gretel)

The smell of baked goods is still in the air, slowly fading away. The feeling of a warm hearth is comforting, beckoning. Behind gray smoke, a heavy iron door swings open. The wood beneath the hearth glows with a dull red, breathing ember.

A story is almost finished baking. The kitchen around the hearth is quite small, covered in fairy floss pink wall paper lined with gingerbread brown molding. Red gumdrop footsteps lead away from the hearth into the living room where the arm of a chair looks as if it has been chewed halfway through. Down the hall, a chocolate brown grandfather clock melts slowly, gob by gob. There in the front entrance only crumbs of the graham cracker door remain. The overly vibrant plants in the garden already wilt without their owner around to care for them. They may look as if they will last forever, but the plants already smell of death.

As the tale tells, an old woman once lived here in the middle of the woods. A place where one can only wonder if they have been led there by a certain sweet smell. But how did she get here? Had she been lured by the scent herself many years ago? Maybe someone had sent her, or quite possibly, she simply appeared out of nowhere.

There were two children who would never learn of Misses Sweets' beginning, even though they lied and told about her end. You may know of their names. They are a bit more famous than Misses Sweet, Hansel and Gretel. I will do my best to tell you all I know, so please do excuse me when I must use other peoples' accounts, I will avoid that route as strongly as possible.

In the dawn of the woods when the trees had fewer rings, the river had less bends, and the town seemed farther away, a wild garden grew in that very spot. Berries of sky blue, apples of luscious red, lemons so sweetly yellow they became sour again, and one fruit that only could grow there, the Tacas Fruit.

Each year the town would send out its ten favorite children for a special festival. The whole town would gather to celebrate how happy things could be and all the blessings they shared all year round. They called it the Fruit Festival. And the happiest children would be sent into the woods to eat the Tacas fruit.

This year, the ten children were picked last but not least the only orphan in the village, they called her Two. The town took care of Two as a whole, each house always leaving a seat open and a spot by the hearth at night just in case the happiest girl in town decided to stop by for the night. She had lived with them all, and in the day time, she enjoyed learning many skills. They believed she was a wonderful pick for one of the favorite ten. They sent the children in order. As they did they told each one in a whisper.

"Eat one sweet Tacas Fruit and you will live the happiest of lives. If you should not eat the whole thing, however, you will be miserable for life," the town Orator would say and pat them on the backside to get them running.

Two was the last child to run off. They ran over the bridge and down the path, following their noses the whole way. They jumped and dashed nimbly through the woods, unstoppable in their task.

When the children arrived, they each picked their fruit in the order they had been sent off. This left Two the last child. She climbed the tree like all the rest and swung up into its high branches. She searched and searched, but there was no tenth fruit.

When Two stuck her head out of the leaves to ask if any other child had taken an extra fruit, none responded. They had all left, leaving nothing but the pits of their fruit behind littered on the ground. Two remembered that if a child were not to eat their fruit, they would most assuredly be a miserable child and thus grow into a miserable adult, so Two waited.

The longer she waited the more she grew used to the woods. She built a small shelter on her own, like she had once watched a farmer build for a lamb. To feed herself she ate of the other fruit from the wild garden. When the season changed twice, she started to build herself a fire on the ground from kindling and dry shrubs. She used rocks the way the blacksmith would to start her own little blaze.

After a few months of living in the woods, her shelter had started to grow and she had made herself a small hearth made of round, flat stones. She had strewn together a bed of leaves and vines.

A year passed and the villagers sadly forgot Two had gone off into the woods as one of the ten children.

This is finally where I enter the story.

I was merely ten years old. I was the adopted son of a lone monk. He was the town's Orator. Yes, he had met Two; he had let her in for meals when she decided she wanted the best bed time story in town. We had slept in the same house, and I can remember even then how wonderfully nice she was.

I, like most of the town, had put her out of my mind as I kept on living my life. My adoptive father taught me how to read, write, pray, sing, and something that would pay off greatly, how to tell stories. My father was Monk Orator, so they called me Little Orator. I lived a simple and happy life. I was always willing to help others. I would do their reading for them, if they needed, in a heartbeat.

There was something that set me apart from the other children of town; I had an odd right foot. I never really even took it into account, but because of that, I seemed twice as happy for the things I was blessed with. I used a crutch to accommodate for my odd foot. I had been using it since I learned how to walk. I was quite fast for being odd footed. I would hate to call it clubbed, so I will not, even though that is what it was.

That year, I was sent off with nine of my school mates whom all excelled in helping their neighbors, just like me.

My father leaned down to my ear and whispered.

"Eat one sweet Tacas Fruit and you will live the happiest of lives. If you should not eat the whole thing, however, you will be miserable for life."

Then he sent me off, as the first one along the journey. I was fast, even with my foot the way it was. I was out of town, over the bridge, and into the woods in no time at all. I was jumping over branches, rushing past hallowed trees, then I was there, the middle of the woods.

I saw the vibrant plants and couldn't help but wonder why it was only the Tacas fruit we were after. I explored the other trees as the other children beat me to the Tacas tree. As I finally made my way over to the Tacas tree, the last of the other kids took off back towards town.

I climbed the tree and began to search its branches. I found no leftover fruit, however. I peeked my head out as high as I could from the tree branches. I saw a little house there with its chimney puffing out smoke. I climbed down from the tree and pushed through the bushes to get a closer look.

The smell was that of candy, freshly baked. I approached and knocked upon the bark door.

"Hello, is anyone here? I was wondering if you might know where I can get a Tacas fruit," I said into the little one room house.

"Hello. Are you the Orator's son?"

"Two? You built this all on your own? The bark door, the stone fireplace and chimney?"

I was amazed at what she had made as she let me in. It wasn't much, but for a small girl to have made it made me feel like it was a castle.

"It is mostly just a kitchen. I spent most of my time in the baker's house. It feels safest for me. I cannot help you; my fruit was missing as well. No extra one ever grew so I guess that means I will live out here."

"Isn't it lonely?"

"Sometimes. But you don't have to stay out here, you can go back. You might want to lie to them about not finding your fruit..."

"I won't lie. I will just tell them a story of how I had to give a gift to the tree in order to get my fruit. I am quite good at telling stories."

"Promise me you will come back. Maybe if you do the tree will sprout two fruit, one for you and one for me."

I left Two behind, looking over my shoulder the whole way back. Sadly, I had to wait a few nights to visit the woods again.

When I found the chance I snuck out the window. I had packed a little bag of supplies for her. I grabbed the bag I had made for her, then headed out over the bridge and into Two's tiny yard. Two was outside her house weaving leaves into a new hat for herself. She ran up and hugged me, excitedly.

"You did come back."

"Did any fruit grow?"

"Not yet. But I am sure one day it will, then we can be happy."

"Till then, I brought you a few things." I took out an axe, a pillow, a needle and thread, a few cups, two plates and a few different kinds of seeds. "How about I bring you supplies every full moon? And when I do, we can check on the tree together."

"Will you stay the night?"

"I cannot tonight, but the nights I can, I will."

After talking a bit more, I noticed it was almost dawn so I bid her farewell.

The next time I returned, the seeds had grown into new plants. They were not the things they should have grown into however. The seeds for wheat turned into small gingerbread trees, the pumpkins had vines of green licorice, the onions were gumdrops, and the potatoes were made of chocolate.

Once a month under the full moon when I heard my father's chanting dim, I would sneak out. I had hidden a pair of clothes and boots in a barn not too far away. After that, I made my way into the woods a basketful of items I had traded for supplies. A pair of mismatched red and white curtains, a full set of copper kitchen utensils. I helped her build a house just out of view of the Tacas tree as time went on.

Many years passed by as we both grew into adults.

One night after my father's chanting had grown quiet. I walked to the front door. I looked toward my father's chair in front of the fireplace. He was there breathing slowly staring at me. I left the door open. I went to his side and held his hand. He had grown into an old man that had lived a long life. He had also sadly enough grown weaker and weaker as the years went on due to a case of pneumonia.

"I know you have been going to see Two all these years, out there in the woods on her own. I know you have protected her like a good man should. For that I shall give you a last gift, and my greatest advice," he said to me.

"Father, please, no. I will be alone if you should go."

"First for my gift," he said, ignoring me. "A proper name like I never had, your name will be Narr." He breathed deeply and I felt as if he had been holding that name in since the day he first saw me.

"Thank you father, but I would rather you fight on please."

"Secondly, you are never alone. Go to her and help her find her way back, she will need you."

With that he breathed one last time. I held him for hours as he laid still. The next day the whole town showed up to help lay him to rest.

I waited till the next full moon and made my way, as always, to Two's little house. I knocked upon her door.

"Two..." I whispered. She did not respond. I knocked again. The door swung open gently and I made my way inside. I had come in so many times, the wonderment that was this candy created house was beyond me. I could smell the sweetness of baking in the air so I made my way into the little kitchen.

Two was there pulling something glorious out of the hearth. She looked at me and smiled tenderly.

"Well, don't you look happy? What is it? You look for too pleasant for, my odd footed boy," she said as I blushed.

"I finally have a name Two. They call me Narr. Come back to the village with me, please."

"I still have never gotten my fruit. I will be unhappy." She turned from me.

"We do not need one. We can be happy together. I am happy with you after all."

"What if a child should arrive hungry? Or one should leave a gift and then come to notice it hasn't been accepted? They will be just as sad as I was."

I could hear how lonely she had always felt.

"Then stay my dear Two and I will come to visit you as always. You are far too kind for children that you do not know."

"The same as the townspeople were to me when I was young."

I understood her. I knew she would never leave that place until her fruit had grown, so she could be happy. I was alright with this because it meant I always knew where she would be, safe in the woods.

In total, sixty years had passed by, not a single fruit grew on the tree that year. Two filled a basket with all the sweetest fruit she could find and left it underneath the tree with a note that read,

"Take this, sweet child, and tell the villagers there is no more fruit to be had, but if any child should ever be hungry enough to wander off, this will be the place they may find comfort and a full belly."

For a few years every spring, Two would still receive gifts in place of her basket of sweets but they were less and less.

One day they stopped coming altogether. After all these years, I had somehow worked my way up to becoming a village elder.

A ceremony was held on the day that the town used to have its Fruit Festival. I told a version of Two's tale. The new tale would hopefully inspire any children who were seeking food or shelter to have hope at the foot of the Tacas tree. At the end, the mayor read a story told by my father that I had never heard about a little boy with an odd foot who grew up to be, not only one of the wisest men in town, but the greatest story teller ever known. A man named Narr Orator. From then on, I had a name. They no longer called me Little.

Everything was going well until, one day, they came. Into the town came storming two of the most famous liars in story telling history. If only I had known what was about to happen, I could have stopped them in their tracks. Hansel and Gretel.

The children caused a fuss wherever they went. The two were kicked out of the school house for eating chalk. They were banned from church for adding their own embellishments to the psalm books. One day, they came to me, father, then mother, then children in tow. The two bickered over the most simple of things.

"They are always hungry and we are as poor as poor can be, please help us, Narr," the mother and father begged.

I felt truly bad for them, so I held a collection. Although most of my townsfolk fought me on the idea, they helped in hopes the children might actually change if help was offered.

Three weeks passed and the family returned. They begged and begged as their children partially destroyed the village hall. I offered the parents work, and they accepted.

Three weeks later, the father hurt his back and the mother believed she was with child again. I attempted to put the children into learning a skill. Both acted halfheartedly in whatever work I gave them, even if it was an easy, joyous task.

First, they only picked weeds when they worked with the gardener. Next they only picked pebbles when they worked with the stonemason. Finally they ate all the sweets at the baker's expense. If they were truly hungry, I knew one person who could fill their appetites. I sent a messenger to summon them to my room at the village hall. Being a helpful man, I set up a plan.

When the family of the infamous siblings returned, I had them sit so I could explain my plan to help them.

"We will do anything, please, Sir Orator."

"Have the children take these," I said and placed two bags full of bread crumbs upon the floor in front of them. "One bag of bread each, go and drop them in the woods as you walk. Leave them as a trail to guide you back. When the bag is empty you should reach a barren tree. Leave this white little bird at the foot of the tree." I made my way into my cupboard and brought them a caged white bird.

"Do not return until you have done as I asked. When you have returned, ring this bell so that we know you are back." I showed them the bell that hung outside of my door. As we watched the two children leave, bags full of bread, and caged bird in hand, their parents turned to me.

"How, sir, might this help us find food?"

"There once was a tree in the wood that grew fruit out that way. If the children leave the tree a gift, it may grow fruit once more."

Then we waited. In silence I prayed. They seemed to pray, I was not quite sure what words their prayers held. When the sun set and the children hadn't returned, their parents went home knowing they would hear the bell would alert them.

Three days passed us by.

An hour before the sun set, the two children came out of the woods covered in dirt, sweating with a look of panic on their faces. Hansel rang the bell feverishly. Their parents and I came to see what had happened. I hoped they had been filled and would no longer be a problem.

"We met a blind old witch. She fed us, and pampered us, and tricked us."

"Tricked you how?" I asked almost dumbfounded. Two had never made a fool out of anyone, nor would she ever want to.

"She was going to bake us. She lived in a house made of candy and sweets. When we placed the bird under the tree we could smell a sweet scent hanging in the air. So we followed it just a little bit farther into the woods. We tried to give her the bread to eat instead," said Gretel.

"But all she wanted on it was slices of Hansel," said the boy.

I gave the family their share of milk and bread. My head was spinning. Something about their story was horribly wrong. What had happened out there in the woods? I did not trust these two any farther than I could throw them. As soon as the children's parents had collected them, I rushed off into the woods as discreetly as possible.

Over the bridge, through the woods, I found myself jumping over the remains of the candy cane fence Two and I had put together. Only crumbs stood where the door had been. I blocked out the candy coated horror scene I found myself in the middle of.

I was on my knees in front of the oven pulling it open in no time at all. I reached my arms in and pulled out what was left of my sweet Two. I could feel her. She was still moving, she felt like unset gelatin. I pulled her into my arms.

"Let me stand" she whispered. So I did. Her skin was the color of licorice. As I walked her through the house her age melted off. I looked at her every two steps turning my head for even a moment to watch. She was eighty, sixty-five, fourth-two, thirty-seven, twenty-one, seventeen, and finally fifteen.

"The children seemed like angels. The boy whistled strongly as he and his sister skipped up to my front door. At first, they claimed they were starving, so I fed them. When my baking and cooking didn't satisfy, I let them eat from the garden, but that didn't do the trick either. They ate for three days straight. Chairs creaked under the boy's heavy body while the girl ate and ate with nothing to show for it. Then things really got out of hand. The boy took a bite out of my arm chair, I protested. The two teamed up on me tied me to a chair and made me watch."

"Watch what?"

"They melted the clock to make hot chocolate. They tore up the fence to bash down the door. When that was devoured they opened up the hearth door, dropped in the pits from the Tacas fruit, and threw me in. As the door slammed shut I felt the heat and heard them vow to return to eat me as well."

"Two, I am so sorry. If they do return I will make sure they cause you no harm."

"It was horrible. I have never known children so spoiled in my life."

"The pits were from the Tacas fruit, you used to collect them?"

"Of course. I was hoping that if I did when the tree buds I could replant them."

"Do you have any more?"

"Of course, I collected them every year."

I had a plan.

After coming out of the woods I saw the two children causing some trouble in the streets. When a villager shooed them away, I followed them. They led me back to their traveling house. It had eight of the healthiest horses I had ever seen, with a two story house built out of a wagon, the house decorated with colors and paints I had never seen.

When I peeked in the window, there was the family, the father was dancing around, the mother holding a baby doll in her hands as the children both tossed food into the air, not caring if it had gone to waste.

Right then and there, I drew a line in the sand. Not only were the children rotten as a pumpkin in January, but the parents were just as bad. I returned to my quarters where I knew the family would come, and waited. Finally Hansel, Gretel, and their horrid parents returned to me.

Again they came in and the children did as they always seemed to do. They caused the biggest mess, and made as much noise as they could. Their parents begged and pleaded.

"Please, greatest Mister Orator, please help us handle our children. We can sense that you are reaching them. They had a break through last night. One more time and we think they might be good," their father said.

"We have run out of bread, they have drank all the milk. We beg of you," their mother said.

"I do not think I can help. They are out of control. I would never say this of any other children, but I think they might do better off in the woods with the wolves," I told them.

"They are but children, and they have nothing to eat. Please, we beg of you to help us, Great Orator. They will do anything you say."

I picked up a bag of stones I had gathered from my garden and placed it on the floor in front of the family.

"Alright, hmm well. Go out with all your pockets filled with stones and do not return until they have been emptied," I said knowing exactly where they would go. The two children did as I said. Their parents helped them fill their pockets with stones knowing bread and milk would come if their task had been finished. As they did so, I left them alone.

I headed out to the woods to beat them out to Two's house. I helped Two hide where they wouldn't be able to find her if they went looking.

The hearth was all prepared with the same number of pits. I could hear the boy's whistling just as Two had described it. I pulled on a hooded tattered cloak, smudging green fruit slime on my face. I readied myself and in they came. The boy ripped off a remaining chunk of the door taking a huge bite of it.

"We are back, Two, to taste you and eat you," he hollered.

"You have spoiled us too well with your sweet ways, lady witch," the girl added in.

I laughed as deeply as I could from the kitchen.

"You children face a bigger, meaner foe," I said, thinking I sounded quite convincing.

"Who goes there?" they said sounding full of themselves.

"Ittle the Unbakeable." Bad name I know, but it did the trick.

"You killed my Two, and now I shall kill you," I said menacingly and walked from the kitchen into the waiting room beside the armchair, a large copper ladle in one hand. I slapped it into my open hand making a thwopping sound.

The two looked me up and down seeing how frail and old I looked, judged this would be no hard task to end me as well. The boy ripped up a rail from the banister and the girl picked up some bobble from a bookcase. I put up a decent fight for being an old man.

Eventually, however, I let them win. They tied me up, opened the hearth and tossed me in. As the door slammed I could hear them.

"We will be back, Ittle the Unbakeable, with the whole village to eat you and Two." A few moments later I heard the door open I could feel Two's arms around me. As I stood, I felt as if the age was melting off of me as it had with her. We walked.

I was eighty-seven now, sixty-two, fifty-six, thirty-one, twenty-four, nineteen, and it stopped at fourteen. She embraced me and smiled that smile I first saw when I met her years ago.

"I never met such horrible children," I said to her.

"I don't think I have ever met such a wonderful man."

"It has been a long time since you have dealt with any other men. Those two will be back and I am sure they will bring a mob. We must be prepared my sweet," I told her, standing up.

"We will have to come up with new names," she replied.

"Mister Sweet and Misses Sweet."

"I love the sound of it."

I smiled at her. The two of us got to work. Our bodies being young again allowed us to move as fast as lightning. I peeked out the window as soon as we had finished cleaning things up and there they were. Just as expected, Hansel and Gretel were coming our way with a group of villagers in tow. The fence didn't have a single lick off of it, the door wasn't missing a single crumb, and its knocker had been placed back in its home. As they knocked we opened the door. We looked young to them, new. Our hands clasped together.

"Hello, we weren't expecting visitors. Look, darling, the whole town seems to have come to visit us," I said and Two smiled.

Hansel and Gretel pushed their way in.

"The clock had been smashed, it was melting…" whined Hansel.

Now, however it was standing upright, ticking away. Hansel trudged on and found Two's armchair where a sugar white doily had been placed over the left arm. Hansel's face had this sickening grin as if he was about to get proof of his tale.

"There was a huge bite out of this armchair. I was forced to eat it," grumbled Hansel. He pulled it up and found the chair was in perfectly good condition. The look on his face was priceless.

Gretel pushed further as the villagers' whispered starting to disapprove of the obvious lies of the two children. The two led the group into the kitchen, which looked as if it had never been the place two children could have ever been held against their will. Nevertheless it looked as if you might have to pull most children out of the room, it smelled so sweet.

"We pushed her in there after we,…" Hansel said pointing to the oven.

"He means after she," Gretel panicked.

"You two have done nothing but tell lies and cause trouble the whole day," said one of the town elders, who Narr recognized, but the same could not be said in reverse.

No one in town believed Hansel and Gretel's side of the story, but still they continued to tell it over and over until no one would listen to a word they said.

They moved soon after to another village, where I am sure they would tell the same tale. I once even heard a version come back about a blind old witch and a boy with a beanstalk or something along those lines. But that isn't what mattered to Two and me. She was young again, and so was I.

That spring we planted one of the pits in the garden, and a tree grew, instantly budding the strange, sweet fruit. Two made a pie out of the Tacas fruit. cutting it into ten slivers. As the smell wafted out into the air, it attracted the ten happiest children from the village. The left over pits when baked again the next day would bring us the rudest children.

This tradition went on for generations, to honor valuing a happy life, and teach those who clearly need it. Not to eat them, as Hansel and Gretel would have loved you to believe, just to have them push us in the oven while it had been filled with the pits of the sweet fruit.

I do hope you'll excuse me now our latest two little helpers have arrived, and Two loves it when I hold open the door. This is the true ending of how Two and Narr lived sweetly ever after.

***

The Singing Man

The children played a game. The children played a game with dolls. The children played a game with dolls down in the basement. In a hole in the wall down in the basement the children played a game with dolls. The game was fun. The game of dolls was about the people in the attic. The game of dolls was fun…until it was almost done.

The two little girls waited till late at night, they snuck out of their bedrooms. The girls made their way along the long hallway and down the stairs. In no time at all there was cold, broken, dusty concrete beneath their unsocked feet. Giggling and whispering, they snuck around the rarely used tool bench. In the back of the basement as far away from light as they could be, the little girls removed a soggy wooden board.

There the cloth dolls waited to play. The dolls were two women, a child and a man. The dolls seemed happy and content in their hole in the wall. The man stayed by the ladder that led downstairs, he came and went as he pleased. He brought the other dolls everything they could ever need or want. He always had a song to sing when he came a-climbing up the ladder.

"This is Singing Man. Here he comes, a-climbing up the ladder," the older sister said.

The Singing Man was the start of all the games, and the end as well. He was how the story was told for the most part. He wore black pants, a white shirt with a black jacket, and a black little tie. He was bald, and wore quite a happy smile on his face.

"What song does he sing tonight, big sister?" asked the younger sister.

In the attic we will stay,

'til the others go away

Let us eat and let us play,

'til the third hour of the day.

"He brought tea for mother, a book for stranger, and sweets for child," the older sister said, making the male doll dance around as his tune echoed through her head.

"And here is child. He is quite hungry from waiting for so long, he waited all day," said younger sister. Younger sister picked up the little boy doll, she lifted him, and brought him over to collect his sweets from the Singing Man.

"There is Stranger in her chair, or is it Mommy Doll with hair so fair?" said older sister. Picking up one of the female dolls she made it sit in a little rocking chair. Then she rocked it back and forth.

"What is stranger's name tonight?" asked younger sister.

"I have no clue. No name ever seems to fit her quite right. Sometimes, I can't even tell which one stranger is. Her and Mommy Doll seem so alike," replied older sister.

"This one will be Stranger tonight, and that one can be Mommy." Younger sister held up the littler cloth doll in one hand with a blue dress on, and waved it around, moving it into the only chair in the little scene. The other doll was tossed to the side for now.

There were two beds, one blue and one green. There was a dresser with its drawers locked shut. There was a rug that hadn't been washed or beat free of dust in quite some time. There was a circular table with three legs, with room enough for three of the dolls to stand around. Last, but not least, there was a little window with white lace curtains that almost could have been made of spider web they seemed so frail. No light came in through the window. It was painted on and made to look as if the time was night.

"What book did he bring for Stranger?" asked older sister as she played with the doll in the rocking chair.

"A book of poems bound in black leather, they rhyme and everything," younger sister said, and placed the little book on the three legged table. As she did, it opened showing its thin little pages.

"I didn't know they had a book that opened," said younger sister.

"It didn't the last few nights," said older sister. A slight breeze came through the basement and turned the white pages.

"It is a special night," younger sister says, picking up the child doll. She tore him away from the sweets that Singing Man had brought. His face was now stained with red, as if he had actually been eating.

"Look, child's tongue is sticking out. It must be time to play the dolls' favorite game."

"Hide and go find me."

All the dolls but child hid their eyes so he could find a spot to hide. He tried to hide behind the curtains, but they found him. He tried to hide under the table, but they found him. He tried to hide under the bed, but they forgot they were playing a game, so they let him stay.

Upstairs there was a noise. The girls turned their heads up toward the floor boards as they heard one set of feet walking away from the family room toward the master bedroom. Their real mother must be headed off to bed.

"Singing Man has checked the ladder, he has peeked on down. He sings again to tell us what all the matter was," older sister said.

One hour gone into the night
 Now the women start to fight.
Where is the child, is it out of sight?
 The others say to run in fright.

"Look, he has brought a pillow so one of the dolls can rest its head," said older sister.

"Well, child's bedtime is coming soon. It is good that the Singing Man is always prepared."

"I want to play Mommy Doll tonight," said older sister.

"You played Mommy Doll last night, I was Stranger. Now it is my turn," said younger sister.

"Stranger gets the book though. We both know the book is way more fun."

"But I want to brush Mommy Doll's hair."

"Alright, you play Mommy Doll. You never play with the book right anyway." Older sister took hold of Stranger and brought her to the window.

Child snuck around her ankles, the red candy stain still smeared all over his little face. Like a little monster, he crawled on all fours from under one bed to the other. Stranger ignored the child and then was brought to the dresser where she seemed to be searching for a key to open its drawers.

The top drawer slid open. Both of the girls tilted their heads but continued to play. Mommy Doll flipped through the pages, Stranger took three items out of the dresser.

Out came a little black candle with its wick already orange from flame. Out came a velvet cloth, so soft it seemed it had been kept for special occasions. Last out came a hand mirror. They moved the table under the window. Mommy Doll and Stranger covered the table in the velvet cloth. They placed the hand mirror reflective side up and placed the candle on top of it.

"Say the words and make it so," younger sister said, holding Mommy Doll and making her walk around the table in circles. Older sister looked closely at the book, as near as she could get. The words were little, but still just legible, one word per page.

"We,…live,…again,…next,…hour,…sleep,…tight,… in,… your,… bed,…just,…to,… dream,… you,… will,… soon,… be,…"

A neighborhood cat screeched nearby the house, startling the two girls. They stopped playing for just a moment and when they looked back, the book was on its last page.

"Dead," said older sister. "It is far too late for Child to be awake," younger sister said, noticing she could not find the child doll.

"Good thing Singing Man brought a pillow. But look, Child is running away. He is playing hide and find me," older sister commented. They turned their heads up as they heard their Father head off to bed. He stopped outside their bedroom and heard a snoring noise. It was not them but he did not know. They could not hear it so on they played.

"He checked the ladder once again, partly to check for Child. But Child had found a bed and made pretend to sleep. He would be back without a sound when the halls were safe."

Two hours passed one more to go.

Hear the clock it clicks so slow.

The others sleeping will never know.

Feel your mind as it overflows.

Up in the master bedroom, the girls' mother and father tossed and turned, both dreaming of the most horrid things.

Within their mother's dreams she saw…

Her two little girls playing out in the yard. The sun shining down as she had never seen it before. They were bending over, chatting about some imaginary thing they had dug up or found on a little adventure by the river. The cedar tree with the swing was close by them. It, however, was not what it should be. It was dead, rotten, not a single leaf clung to its branches. Bees surrounded it in giant swarms, going in and out of giant holes that appeared as the tree fell apart around the two girls. Night came fast as four moons rose into the sky. She was there, her little baby girls still playing as if nothing had happened. When she went to see what it was they had been talking about, in front of them was the doll of the Singing Man. She could hear his song, she knew it was a vile one. She could not wake

Within their father's dreams he saw…

His sister that he hadn't seen in twelve long years. A stranger, but not quite at the same time. The two were reunited in a long dark tunnel. Water dripped through the tiles above them as he could hear the rattling of subway trains not too far away. He was helping her dress in all black. It was the same thing she wore when she stormed out of their parents' funeral. He turned from his sister fast, not wanting to know why she had returned. Issues had never been settled between the two of them. When he turned, he was surrounded by a ballroom. The room filled with tables each ready for a feast, thousands of tables all gleaming in decadence. Each table had three lamps, all flickering dimly, waiting for its guests to arrive. In came the guests, all women veiled in white. Instead of walking, they hovered. Filling every single table. The last two in the room lifted their veils. They had the faces of mother doll and stranger doll. He could hear them whispering their spell, word by word. He wanted to run, he wanted to wake, but it was too late.

Back in the basement, hands deep within the hole in the wall, the two girls had just put Child down to bed, tucking him in nice and tight. They had read him a story and sung him a song.

"I do not want to go to bed. I want to play one last time," younger sister said, making him jump around the little room.

"Only if Stranger's spell is ready," older sister said, helping the Singing Man try to wrangle Child.

"It has been spoken, it has been read. Mother and Father are well off to bed," Stranger said, now being moved around the little house.

"He will check the ladder one last time to see if all is well. Then he will cast Stranger's horrid spell," older sister said.

Last hour gone the time has passed.

Those playing and sleeping will tremble fast.

Our spell, our song, our curse has been cast.

For here we come down the ladder at last.

They froze in place as they heard it from all the way upstairs. They could hear the attic door swing open from the ceiling. It made so much noise, with all its springs creaking and stretching. But their parents did not wake, they were too caught up in those horridly repetitive dreams.

Finally, they could hear the wooden ladder make impact on the carpeted floor, dust coming from both bodies. An unstoppable force meeting an immovable object. Then one pair of little feet rushing down the ladder. One pair of black heeled feet, then another.

Finally, they could hear the creak as the last set of feet came down with a hum to match his decent. All the feet walked down the hall to the master bedroom. The door slammed open.

All the girls could hear was the Singing Man, as he sang a new song they had never heard before. They were forced to listen as his song repeated itself four times. Then the parade of feet made its way, in order, passed their bedroom, passed the family room, and through the kitchen. There was only one room left the people from the attic had not visited.

The basement door swung open and the Singing Man's song filled the air louder than ever before.

In the silence now we wait.

Till once again it becomes too late.

Another song, another trap, another date.

Two mothers, two fathers, three children and a stranger all

too eager to anticipate.

***

A Writer's Life

The doctor came into the waiting room. It was three AM, the night was growing long.

"Mr. Kolasar?" the doctor said to the only man sitting there.

The man had bonded himself to an open composition notebook via a plastic pen. Mr. Kolasar had buried himself so deep into his scribbling he had lost track of the world around him. He had been doing this since he was ten years old.

"That's me. Please, just James, though."

"James, I have good news."

"Really? Is she?" he said breathless.

"Right this way. She is ready for you." The doctor waved his hand.

They walked down the hallway. James clutched his notebook so tight that the pen, which he had placed in its pages, had exploded.

There were pages currently soaking in every last drop of ink. James had filled the notebook with words for this moment. In fact, he had filled nine notebooks for this moment, this one being the most current. The doctor stopped in front of room B248. The doctor grinned.

"Ready?"

"I don't know if I will ever be ready. I have been waiting so long."

"We all think that, don't worry." The doctor opened the door.

"You will make a great father." James walked into the small hospital room. Inside, another man about James's age stood smiling, holding a little ball of pink blankets. The other man looked up.

"She is…" the other man said.

James rushed over. He joined his husband.

"She looks like a little bird. Little Robin. Our little girl." They held her, passing her between each other.

Hours passed, days, years… as they always do. James filled books, he won awards, toured the country, and always came back.

One day, James stepped out of his home office. There on the floor in the sunlight was his seven year old daughter, Robin.

Notebook paper surrounded her on the floor, she had written the words she could over and over. James looked up as Brian came out from the kitchen.

"Honey, enough writing for today. Come help me set the table for dinner."

"Which one of us are you talking to?" James replied.

"Why don't you both help?" Brian responded.

James stomped down the hall. He picked up Robin, tossing her over his shoulder as he made the noise of some huge dinosaur. She faked a scream and giggled all the way to the dining room. The family set the dinner table, Robin bounced away to another room.

"How long was she on the floor writing like that for?" James asked.

"Most of the day. She reminds me of you. Maybe she will go on book tours, father and daughter one day?" Brian paused he looked at James's face. "What's wrong?"

"It's hard to be a writer. It doesn't always end happily."

"Our story is going quite well."

"People will think she's strange, sometimes she'll create from nowhere and it will confuse her and scare her."

34

"So, she is just like you?" Brian mocked gently. "I am kidding. She will have a wonderful pair of parents to help her out. When the ink spills, we will help her clean it. Plus, one day, she can tell your story. That is the life of a writer, right?" Brian smiled.

James grinned, giving in, knowing Brian was right. James would be there no matter what. The two finished preparing dinner and called their daughter down to eat. A family, no matter how strange they might seem.

***

Zena and the Deep Wood

Zena Jumble pulled on her glittering, golden one-button sports coat. Pulling out a lint roller, she rolled it up and down the coat sleeves. She rolled the lint roller over the crest, over her heart.

The crest over her heart was a red cap mushroom that had a small wooden door and two open windows. Her hair was combed; she had her briefcase packed the night before. Inside awaited the comps for houses in the Underbrush District of Deep Woods.

Zena placed her pen into her pocket and made her way outside. She was ready for her first open house. She walked along the porch of her little colonial style bird house, flexed her lilac fairy wings, and took off.

She flew up first through the Nest End Heights, then across Meadow Park. She landed at the real estate office, which was housed among the Mushrooms of Down River Glen. She properly adjusted her size so she could fit into the door.

Her colleagues were sitting at their desks, getting their files ready. She grabbed two sets of keys from her desk and left the real estate agency.

A few moments later, after gliding south of Down River, she finally reached Forest's Edge. She would have to either take the underground Mole tunnels from here or walk. She had luckily pulled a few extra acorns from her jar for lunch that day. She walked to the nearest molehill, sliding down inside.

As the light of day faded, the dull glow of the underground tunnels grew a bit brighter. A few elf police officers waited down the platform, as well as some pixie baby sitters. Each had placed their acorns into the toll booths as they entered the station. Zena dropped her acorns into the toll slot. She watched them wiz up and around the tubes in order to summon the right amount of moles.

37

A moment later, five moles arrived, pulling little carts behind them. Zena hopped in the last mole cart, zooming away down the dark tunnel. She passed four stations, finally getting out at Deep Woods.

She made her way up into the dimly lit district. It was not the best place to walk alone at night. The roots had risen up here and had become home to many of the creepy crawly creatures that most flying creatures avoided at all costs. She walked along the leaf lined roads.

Finally, she found the house she would be showing today. Ninety Two Ivy Way, at the corner of Pillbug Plaza. She had planned to meet her first clients, the Browns, here. She entered the twig fence gate, walking up the pebbles towards the three-story Sticktorian Classic style house. She unlocked the door and walked inside.

Everything was all set. The pillows were fluffed, the shelves were dusted. She put on her best smile and waited. Her boss had told her she was getting quite the high end client for her first house tour. After that, it would become an open house so the Browns would see the house would sell. She walked out into the little yard.

She pulled some fairy dust from her pocket. She blew the dust making a "For Sale" sign appear out of midair. She crossed her arms briefly, unfolding them when she saw a silkworm strewn carriage pulling down the street.

The mouse driver hopped off the front of the carriage. The driver opened the carriage door and out came a couple that Zena had seen many times before. Their faces were plastered on billboards, magazines and all over the gossip news. Mr. and Mrs. Brown were none other than Aracus Jo Leech and Lady BugBug. Two of the world's most loved musicians that had run away to a secret wedding, and now were looking for a place to settle down and raise a family.

Zena waved gently, acting as normally as she could. She had made it, and her dreams were coming true. She was more than just a real estate agent, she was one for the rich and famous.

***

Eliza in Disguise

Eliza Newson did not look like herself when she emerged from her cross-dressing best friend's apartment. Passing by a mirror in the hall made her flinch. No matter how unnerving this felt to her, it was for a good cause. She had been dreaming of being Eliza Newson-Durberry for three years now.

Two weeks ago, her fiancé, Harold, had begun to act somewhat uncharacteristic. His work schedule had not increased, but his commute had grown longer and the times he never made it passed the couch to the bed quadrupled. The bells in her head had started to go off. What if there was another woman involved? What if he had another life on the side she had never caught onto? She had to do something to make sure he was not cheating on her. This is where her plan of disguising herself and doing a little bit of spying rose up.

After sitting in her car for half an hour making phone calls to every place she thought Harold might be, as she had done for the last two days, she drove down to his office. Every time she looked in the rear view mirror, she had to check the backseat for someone who might look more like herself.

Everything about her was wrong. The brunette curly wig over her short black bob cut, the green contacts over her naturally brown eyes, even her cheekbones seemed out of place.

When she arrived at Harold's office she stormed right up to his secretary. She demanded to see Harold.

"He is out, Ma'am. On a business meeting."

"I made an appointment," Eliza said truthfully, having planned this out.

The girl curled her finger, drawing Eliza close so she could whisper something.

"He is down at St. Johns Hospital on 17th, if you really need his attention that badly," the secretary said.

Eliza was stunned.

"Couldn't you get fired for telling me that?"

"I hate this job. What do I care? Plus, my horoscope said to be helpful to the elderly. So there we go, you got me my karma merit badge for the day," the girl said.

Eliza was infuriated, but did not have the time to express it. She rushed out of the office. She was only twenty nine and was by no means elderly, but as she caught her own reflection yet again, she realized her costume was working after all.

She drove all the way down to 17th street, pulling into the parking lot. Not a single red light on the way, fate was on her side. She passed Harold's car, then parked as far away from it as she could. Hustling into the hospital, she was like a tornado.

A male nurse sat at the greeter's desk. He looked as if he had been badly beaten as a child, and or he was just born ugly. As he opened his mouth Eliza noticed four or five missing teeth.

"May I help you, Ma'am?"

"Did a Harold Durberry sign in?"

"Are you a family member?"

"Yes. Well, I will be. We are getting married in June."

"Can I see your license, Ma'am?"

"Yes." She pulled out her driver's license. Suddenly, it clicked in her head she looked nothing like the photo.

The male nurse pushed a button and two security guards came over. They took her arm and led her down the hallway, passing many open doors.

Number 17 was open and as she passed, she saw her husband to be. Harold was sitting next to an old woman, his grandmother. Eliza's mind sparked. Harold's grandmother had been sick for some time now and Eliza, for some reason or another, had blocked out Harold mentioning he was going to be visiting her. He had told her the doctors said she didn't have much time left. Guilt consumed Eliza as she told her story to the guards, a story her fiancé would not hear for a good thirty years.

***

Fight or Flight

"I can see it in your eyes, the panic. What's gotten you so scared?" Bruce, one of the two middle school aged boys, said.

The two boys sat on a bench, the door to the principal's office no more than four steps away. The other boy sat silently staring down at his dress sneakers. The other boy's right shoe had left a trail of red footprints all the way down the hall.

"Oh, it can't be that bad, Taylor?" Bruce said. Bruce looked at Taylor sitting there, visibly shaken. They both were dressed the same; white dress shirts, black dress pants, belt with silver plated buckles, and ties with green and gold stripes. The halls, much like Taylor, remained completely silent. It was the middle of the fourth period classes. It was a small school for all boys, so most of the kids knew each other by name, but just big enough for a few of the weaker, smaller boys to still fall through the cracks and get picked on here and there.

"Wait, was it you all the other kids were calling Teller? You were the one that told on Cam for writing on the walls in the bathroom."

"I am afraid of birds, and he was writing it on the walls," Taylor mumbled.

"What did you say?" Bruce said, honestly not hearing him.

"He was writing about me. He knew I have a fear of birds. But I got him back. I did it. I destroyed his stupid mockup of a red robin. I enjoyed as I watched the red paint pool underneath my shoe. Like a boot on a worm, finally I got him back for years of bullying." Taylor stood from the bench. He was breathing heavily, his chest heaving, his hair blew off of his face when he sent a huff of air out his mouth. He stomped his right foot down with every other word, leaving a thicker mark of red upon the once white tile flooring.

The door to the principal's office opened. Principle Wintey poked her head out and nodded for Bruce to come in. Bruce silently and slowly stood up, carefully making his way into the principal's office, trying not to catch Taylor's eye.

Taylor took a deep breath, finally alone. He had stood up for himself. He sat back down, a bit proud and ready to accept his punishment.

***

The Wet Book

Keira's sneakers were soaked as soaked could be, she practically left puddles as she stepped into her house. Her mother looked at her for a moment. Her mother slowly tilted her head as her mind wondered about something quite peculiar. There hadn't been a drop of rain in three weeks now. They didn't live by any lakes, rivers, or anything of that sort.

"Keira?"

"Yeah, Mom?"

"How did your shoes get so wet?"

Keira looked at her mom while giggling, knowing she would never for a moment believe the story she was about to tell.

Her wet shoes had been dry when she started out on just a simple walk in the warm spring sun. She was headed to the library. Keira had simply wanted to pick a good book for a quick read. She was that kind of a young woman. Always finding her way into other worlds through the pages of books. It was one of the many amazing things about Keira.

She turned the block toward the library when dark clouds filled the sky above her. She had never seen clouds quite so dark before. She looked over at the fountain in front of the library. The water within it looked deeper than she had ever seen it. She leaned over the fountain when it burst into millions of pieces. Water rushed around her ankles. A little wooden ship that some child had left behind grew into quite a large schooner. Its sails billowed in the wind.

"Help me, my ship is under siege." A voice came from the open deck of the ship.

"I can help." She beckoned, still only ankle deep within the waves.

A sailor popped his head over the side of the ship. He smiled, grateful for any helping hand. He threw down a rope ladder for her to climb up. Keira quickly scaled the ladder.

"Please, lil' lass, help me rid my ship of this horrid sea beast," the sailor said, as soon as she was on deck.

A great purple and orange sea beast, with long slimy tentacles, had come in through the sailor's cabin window. It had started to push its way out of the door and onto the open deck.

"Block the door," she told the sailor.

He placed his body in front of the cabin door. She reached deep into her bag, her whole right arm vanishing deep within. Out she pulled her pen. She quickly pulled out a piece of paper. Keira sketched a drawing of a sword pen, quickly wrapping the paper around the pen. A second later she was holding a pen sword. She had a proud look on her face.

"How miraculous? What magic is this?" the sailor asked.

"The power of ink," Keira said, parrying the pen sword forward. "Open it up, I will finish with the sea beast in no time at all."

The sailor swung open the door.

Keira held her pen of a sword up steadily. She quickly drew as fast as she could. She traced iron shackles around each of the sea beast's slimy tentacles. Quickly, she drew a key for the shackles as well.

"Beast, if you leave this ship now, I will let you have this key to free yourself. Otherwise, I will toss it to the bottom of the sea. It will take you a long time to find it down there, now you don't want that do you?" Keira said smartly.

The beast pulled itself out the back window, closing them behind itself. Keira sighed lightly.

She ran to the side of the ship, watching for the beast. All she saw was the tip of one of its many tentacles pop out of the water. She tossed the key down.

"For saving me and my ship, I will write your adventure down. That way all will know of how wonderful you are."

She smiled at the sailor. She waited outside his cabin, she paced the deck. Pretending to be a swashbuckler with her pen sword. He came out with a leather book in hand and gave it to her.

"Make sure to bring this back, lil' lass. It has a home here, just as much as it will in your heart."

"Yes sir, captain sir."

"I be only a sailor, lil' lass."

"And I am but a little girl in sneakers that just thwarted off a great sea beast. You will be a captain yet, or a writer, or a potato farmer. That it is up to you." She shrugged him off.

Keira made her way back down the rope ladder as the ship shrank back to its toy size. The clouds parted and the fountain rebuilt itself. Keira told her mother all while she held her pen like a sword.

"That is a cute story, honey, but really, how in the world did your shoes get that wet?"

"Don't believe me, Mom? You can read about it in my book. The sailor wrote it all down. Plus how else would my shoes have gotten so wet?"

She pulled a leather bound book from her book bag. The air filled with the smell of the sea. She placed it on her mother's lap. She sat on the floor and pulled off one shoe, then the other. She smiled as she pulled a piece of seaweed out of her right shoe. She waved it in the air then ran up to her room, ready for all the adventures her books held.

***

The Trail of Two Brothers

"You came all this way just for college?" Cody said to his little brother.

Cody looked around himself. He breathed deeper than he had in a long time. They had been hiking in silence for the last hour. Marky had his faithful red backpack strapped on. It was full of anything they could need.

"Best school for a degree in Forestry. I already do tours out of the trail center. Running my own scouts program to help kids learn the do's and don'ts of the woods."

"Lil bro, there isn't even cell phone reception out here."

"Don't need it." Marky smiled.

"You're happy here, right?"

"Happiest I have ever been. What about you?"

"Here, no, I am going insane out here. Good thing I am only here for four days."

"Why did you come all the way up to Alaska anyway?" Marky asked as he peered through a pair of binoculars he had been wearing around his neck.

"Well, if you really want to know, you can't tell. Ok?"

"Brother's bond? It's been a few years since we shared a good secret."

"Remember Judith?"

"The girl with the dogs? Didn't you two break up?" Marky finally put his binoculars down.

"Well, I went and apologized. We have been seeing each other. I think she might be the one."

"Are you telling me you are going to pop the question?"

"I am terrified of marriage, look at our family. I mean, who is left together, besides Mom and Dad?" Cody asked.

"Aren't they enough?"

"They should be."

"You know there is this trail down in Ketchikan. It leads from the historic red light district."

"Historical prostitutes, really? You are going to use a place like that to make me feel more secure?"

"It leads away from the, yes, historical prostitutes."

"So, there is more to your little story."

"Yes, Cody, the trail starts off with about forty steps. Every five or so is a little platform. It's a pretty steep climb. Then it flattens out and you can see the snowcapped mountains just beyond the trees. I found some berries there. They looked delicious, but I knew better.

All along the way are little off shoots into the brush that lead to nowhere. If you can remain on the well walked path, you will find a stone wall. Men have left their mark there, spray paint mostly.

Then a moment later, at the very top, all the trees clear. You can see it all. Most beautiful thing in the world..."

"Ok, and?"

"Commitment is a steep climb, it is a struggle. If you can look beyond the temptations, the go nowhere paths, you can see that off in the distance the beauty of your journey will grow. The marks of other men will show you that you are so close. Then you get the gold. You get the view and you are no longer alone."

"So you will be saving that little speech as my best man right?"

"You are going to get married? Serious?"

"As serious as you are about this whole wilderness thing," Cody replied.

Brian smiled at him and they both stayed there, enjoying the wilderness for a few moments more. They knew both of their lives were headed in the right direction.

***

Picture of a Man that Couldn't

They once called me Hugo Jones. That was when I had lived here in London, twelve years ago. I lived four blocks away from where I sit now. My sign reads "Can afford food, not love." My jeans are torn over my strong legs. A nice, warm wool coat is covering my flannel shirt, and under my arm, my guitar rests. My fingers caressing its strings like they once caressed the only woman's skin I have ever loved.

I couldn't stay then, no matter how much I wanted to. I loved her every day I knew her. When I went away, I wrote her letter after letter. I called her. I fell in love, somehow more while I was away. I wrote her songs, some so strong, I could not write words for them.

Ten years ago, we walked by the school in front of me now. We talked about the children we would one day love to have. I could not stay for her, never the less for the little ones I was sure she would raise. Imagine me then, passing a man like me now. Not knowing I couldn't yet.

The school bell rings today, just the same as all the others before this one. I see him, eleven years old, I play his song. A fast strum of changing cords, with the same chorus, one so close to hers that I can barely tell the two apart sometimes. He looks over, as he always does. I do not think he knows.

My hair was a crew cut in any photos she had taken with me. I was much more fit back then, a military man. He leans against the school fence in his black coat. James, taps his foot to my music. I can see its cords playing in his very soul.

There she appears, from around the corner. Her brown hair hanging straight down to her shoulders. She is wearing a new coat. One I am sure blocks out every last attempt this cold wind sends her way. She looks the same as she used to those long ten years ago. She never looks at me. We still write letters every week.

"Dear Felicia," I have written her name so many times I do not have to look when I write it. I have the letters forwarded a block the other way, to a dingy little flat with half of a window.

Ten years ago, I vowed as I was being sent to fight, that I would support her no matter what. I send her all that I can. She writes about him like she used to write about me. We both know that I lost something, however, while I was away.

For seven years, I tried to find what that something was, without luck. I am closer to home than I have ever been. I will never tell them though, the last time I said I wanted to have a home was with her, and then I had to go away. War does that, it moves men, it changes countries, and it takes love away. If I can stay silent, then maybe I can stay.

***

An Aging Dream

Laura was a now thirty-something '90s teen, and she finally had achieved that ultimate '90s teen dream; to live close enough to walk to the mall. Her first house, with its little yard for her dog to run around in, and its porch to lay out in the sun on, was only a four minute walk from the mall. Laura pulled on her tennis shoes and jogged over right as the stores were opening. Her feet carried her into the cool, shaded air condition of a place she once considered to be as close to heaven as she would ever get.

It had been quite some time since the '90s, however. What once was a glittering, clean popular hangout was now more than half closed down stores. She walked passed a dried up duck pond with an island in the center, where thousands of kids had once taken pictures with Santa and the Easter Bunny. The bridge to the little island was gated off and locked.

Laura turned away from the duck pond to go the other way. Her favorite store of all time was on the other side of the mall. She had read about a 50% off sale going on. She walked passed an ice cream booth were a teenager sat on his cell phone, not even raising an eyebrow as she passed him by.

A store, much like the one where all the coolest teens once got their clothes, was now strictly a holiday store that had opened two days ago and would surely be closed by the end of the month. It had a "No Returns" policy sign out front, warning that all purchases were final. Laura sighed.

She would pass the candle store, the shoe store and the entrance of the movie theatres. The posters for the movies playing were all way passed their premier dates. One of them advertised for a movie she had gone to see at least eleven years ago.

Right before she could step into the mall's anchor store, a worker from the book store popped out. He had a sandwich board on that advertised for the new digital book reading device, and how it would never give you a papercut. Laura tilted her head a bit and moved passed him.

The store, her favorite store, was just as bad as the rest of the mall, if not worse. The mannequins were all half-dressed, some were missing limbs, or heads. The shelves of purses and shoes that once shone like diamonds were now covered in dust.

She rushed to the Dresses department up a broken down escalator. There it was, the dress that had been made exclusively by some high end designer she could not, for the life of herself, remember the name of. She grabbed a hold of it, she hugged it close to her body, and then suddenly, Laura could not let go. Her arms were locked in an embrace with the black skinny dress. She tried not to smile, but realized all she could do was keep on the sickening grin she had put on when she had pulled the dress off its rack. Laura went to step back from the rack but her feet would not move. As she breathed faster her eyes stopped blinking, her gaze now locked on the dress for eternity.

Laura heard the fire alarms going off around her and felt the sprinklers being turned on. People rushed around her. She tried so hard to blink. The dress still holding her there in this very spot.

Laura awoke. It was 1998. Her bedroom window was open and the sprinkler outside was spritzing a stream of water in at her. Her alarm clock was blaring out for her to turn it off. She breathed a sigh of relief.

***

Noir and Blanc Cookie

There I was again, another case had been solved. I took off my gray fedora with the little yellow canary feather in it. I placed it on the wooden coat holder in my office. Below it hung my gray, still damp from the rain, trench coat.

I flipped the sign on my door. The gumshoe, was in. Open for service, ready to deduce. I peeked my head out and looked at my assistant. She sat there, chewing her gum and wrapping a pencil in her hair as she easily solved quantum physics level math problems, like a child level crossword.

"If someone comes in, let them on in, alright?" I said to her.

"Sounds good, boss," she said back at me, not even looking up.

I made my way over to the one window in my office. Outside, a bright red fluorescent light twitched on and off. I adjusted the blinds, blocking it out as best as I could.

I adjusted my suspender and tie. Turned to my desk and saw it, a black and white cookie sitting on my desk. I had not been the one who left it there. Someone must have known that black and white cookies were my favorite.

I leaned down over it and inhaled. It smelled as if it were still cooling after a perfect session in the oven. I knew it wasn't my secretary, she was the one woman in my life who cared about my health, and she knew the doc had said to cut down on the sugar.

I pulled my chair up, and then rolled up my sleeves. I picked the cookie up. It was soft as a blanket. I could not sense any kind of poison or tampering that this fantastic looking baked good might have endured, so I leaned back. I put my well-polished black leather shoes up on my desk. A few of my folders fell off. I could pick them up later, first I had to deal with this sweet treat that waited in my right hand.

I took a nice, big bite. I bit the cookie right where the line separated the cookie between black and white. Then I took a bite out of just the white side. After that, I bit the black side. So on and so forth, until I was licking my fingers, like a dog licks a bone.

I picked up the cup of coffee I had put down before I had hung up my coat. I realized something horrible. Worst crime I had ever seen. My coffee had been drank. I could still feel the morsels of cookie in my mouth. What a horrible day for a loose cannon detective, one I will never forget.

***

The Mountains of My Family

I had always wanted to visit the windy mountains of Romania, where my family had come from generations ago. I was thirty five and this had been on my list of "must do's". I stood on a precipice with my guide behind me urging me to imagine the warriors that used to call this land home. In the distance, I could see our destination.

A long, stone staircase carved into a mountain not far away. At the top was a small fortress, my heritage waited beyond its wooden door. We spent the next day hiking and as the sun set, we finally reached the base of the stone stairs. There had been a road we could have taken to get there, but where is the fun in that. None of the people I knew could say they had hiked these mountains, never the less a five day trek this far from home.

I had grown up in a Midwest state where a mountain was literally a molehill. The idea of adventure to those small town folks I grew up with was usually something way easier than what my guide and me had been through. We climbed the staircase as the sky turned a mix of orange and purple.

"Go on, knock," my tour guide said with her thick accent.

I rested my hand upon the wooden double doors for a moment. Then I made a fist and knocked. I could hear the echo on the other side of the door. My Uncle Marius opened the door, smiling. He was a tall brute of a man. One who I had heard legends about. Apparently, once he carried a pregnant horse for a half mile.

"Welcome, we have been waiting. You should have been here last night, what happened?" he said, sounding more French than anything else. He had grown up in boarding schools so only his name and his love for Romanian foods held any resemblance to our heritage.

We placed our gear down in a little alcove hidden away. I guessed the alcove might once have been servant's quarters. After seeing all four floors, thirteen bedrooms, the library, the war room, and the chapel; we finally made it to the kitchens. I honestly don't think I will ever know how my uncle and his small family keep the place maintained on their own, but it was beautiful. Aunt Roxanna came out of the pantry as we explored the kitchens.

"It is about time, I was scared all my cooking would be for not," she said.

There was that accent I had been waiting to hear from more than just my guide. She had baked us some of my favorite recipes. The same ones they had been cooking since the Turks tried to destroy this fortress during the dark ages.

Once loved, always loved. Uncle Marius, Aunt Roxanna, my guide and I ate for three hours straight. We ate and ate until the serving plates were stranded in a sea of napkins and used silverware. We stayed up until the sun had almost taken its place back in the sky. I was sure of one thing. I was home. No matter how long ago this had been made, these mountains were the home of my family.

***

The Reaper's Gardener

I watch a burly man sweat as he labors away in the hot sun. He keeps his head down as his spade digs the earth up upon itself. I know he is digging for me. How could two men, such as him and me, be so far from each other, and yet still have something in common?

Him a Gravedigger, me a Duke. I have all that a man could ever ask for, riches, comforts, never an empty stomach when I lay my head to rest. Him, he has a name, a hut, seven children and a way of life that most would never think about twice. He loosens the soil, moves it out, and digs our deathbeds. Then when the hole is made a home, he fills it back in moving on.

His name I don't think I will ever know. I lay here in my bed with more pillows than his head has ever dreamed of. He digs. His shirt, unlike mine, was never truly white. His shirt was always the color of tea and every day he wears it is steeped deeper with the earth's essence.

I watch him from my sick bed, as the Reaper comes from so far away. This man that grows stronger and sweats harder than any other that I have ever watched. His work is such a force of labor I feel as if he could put entire armies to shame. The strength it takes to place more than seventy men beneath the earth is stronger than one needs to send those same men to war. When a Duke such as I sends those men to fight for his land and his brothers' kingdom, he has hope those men can come back. Those men can be victorious, and it is the Duke's memory in the mind of those men that grows fonder when they do. It is those men's faults when they do fail, never the Duke's.

The Gravedigger on the other hand, how can he have such hope? If he hopes those men the best then his families' lives are at stake. By the time he meets these men, they have been vanquished. He measures them using a type of measurement that is unique and under used. He knows my height by the look of me lying in my bed. He knows my weight by the way my mattress sags. I see his wooden outline around the hole he digs. I could lay within it like I lay upon these soiled sheets. Never to roll over again.

I watch him in his muddy shirt as the rain washes him off, his huge strong body steaming. He pulls up the last pound of dirt. He places it in the pile, there with the rest of the earth he removed. The hole is taller than I am. He stands still and slowly looks up right into my window. He nods his head respectfully. After that he gestures to the roses, to the lilies and the daises. He makes sure to show me the lilac bushes, as well as the baby's breath. The flowers and the gardens that were planted for me and my kin lie between me and him. I now see him as more than just a gravedigger, he is the Reaper's Gardener and he's going to carefully plant me. He is going to put me in like every other man, child, or woman; a seed to grow into the next life.

***

Coral Cog's Metallic Mermaid

Hannah brushed her teeth, facing into her bathroom mirror. Today was the day, she was going to get the gift from her Great Aunt Jones. She placed down her tooth brush, spat, and rinsed. Hannah walked toward her bedroom when suddenly the doorbell rang. Hannah took off running like she was twelve years old all over again. She was turning thirty in just two days from now; she had been waiting for most of her life for one gift.

Hannah opened the door to find a deliveryman in all brown standing there.

"Mrs. Hannah Ishanman?" he asked.

"That's me!" she eecked out.

The delivery man took out a pad and a pen, letting Hannah sign for her package. He turned around and carted over a wooden crate a little bit shorter than Hannah. He wheeled the crate into the house and laid it down on the floor.

"Enjoy." He grinned and closed the door behind himself.

Hannah had been prepared, she picked up a crowbar from the coffee table and began prying nails out of the box's lid. In no time at all, the lid was off. Hannah brushed away balls of newspaper.

There she was, her tail made of copper scales glistening, some already greening with years of life. Her skin was smooth metal, as realistic as it could ever be. Hannah caressed her cheek gently. Memories flashing back of being seven years old and finding this very creature in her Great Aunt's tub. A relic of some circus that had come into her life and mysteriously vanished leaving this behind in their tracks.

She unfolded the hand written instructions.

"Twist left pinky once right to active Coral Cog's Metallic Mermaid. Twist left when you wish to turn her off."

Hannah bent down and twisted the Mermaid's left pinky, right, once. Coral Cog's Metallic Mermaid's lips moved. She blinked. Her chest full of breath. She was as real as Hannah in an instant.

Hannah carried her to the tub as gently as possible. She could feel the creature's cogs stirring beneath her cold metal skin. Hannah so wanted to see the Mermaid's tail beneath the water, she had for so long wanted to see it move as if she was there in the ocean itself. Hannah reached for the faucet as she glanced at the Mermaid's sweet face. The Mermaid shook her head, her eyes begging Hannah not to. Hannah thought back to all the times she had snuck away to see the Mermaid in Great Aunt Jones's house, not once had the tub had a single drop of water within it.

Hannah withdrew her hand from the tap not turning it. She knew her one wish would never come true, but now she had another. She would let her niece Beth discover the Mermaid. She would let her be found over and over with never a single drop of water and one day she would send her Coral Cog's Metallic Mermaid, and she would do the same for a niece of hers, so on and so forth.

***

Just in Case: a Story Not in Space

"Yes, I was there. If you don't tell anyone, I will tell you what really happened. It started about five months before the twenty first of July, 1969," Mary Donahue said from an antique armchair.

Fifty-five years had passed by since the moon landing. I was doing research for my final college paper. My project was find someone connected to a world changing event. Luckily for me, I had lived down the block from Mary. I had heard from my parents many times that she was somehow connected to the moon landing. Beyond that, I had never heard how.

So I made my way over to her house one weekend. I found myself on her plastic coated couch with a glass of lemonade in my hand, listening to a story not in space.

"My father was a set designer. He had been brought in by N.A.S.A itself. I went to the set with him twice a week. One day before rehearsal, I was copying the actor who was playing Armstrong. He was late that day and they wanted to make sure the lighting was just right. So they let me run in the sand in slow motion.

"One small step for man, one giant leap for mankind," I said as I leapt around in the sand. My father was sitting by the director. The moon landing was scheduled only another few days away.

"No, honey. The line is simply, one small step for man," my father beckoned out.

"It flows pretty well, almost like a slogan. Where have you been hiding her?" the director said patting my farther on the back. That is how they got the line. Little me in my pigtails, pretty much playing around."

"So, there was a set for the moon landing?"

"Of course there was. It was in a huge warehouse in Florida. Imagine that the astronauts had not been able to land

67

on the moon. The country was so wrapped up in beating the Soviet Union to the Moon that if it had not have happened, we may have had to go to war. I remember all the men talking about beating the Russians, no matter what the cost."

"Even if that meant faking the moon landing?"

"It was necessary. That is why they were all there in that stuffy warehouse with no air conditioning or anything of the sort. I remember the day they brought in the rigging system so the astronauts could bound around easier. They also brought in these big fans to cool off. And my father would always tell me that I could be a part of history."

"Are you telling me the moon landing was actually a hoax?"

"No, it happened. I remember sitting there on set, the man who was playing Neil Armstrong was all dressed up and ready. He had me on his lap as we watched the real Armstrong take his first steps. In fact, the next day before the set was taken apart, I was allowed to play around in the sand. I climbed up on the fake moon lander and everything. We all watched the real thing. We cheered and celebrated with the rest of the country. I took a big bow when the real Mr. Armstrong said my words. Does that help with your paper?"

"That is an amazing story, you get to be the girl behind a backup conspiracy." I smiled and thanked her. Afterward, we talked on about a few other things, but nothing will ever make a better story to me for a paper than the little girl that inspired one of America's quotes.

***

At The End.
(Lucas &Noah)

On a hot summer day, up on the roof of an apartment building, Lucas and Noah had been glaring down at the people, like the people were ants. They had been silent for the last half hour as the world around them fell apart.

"Talk for fuck's sake," Noah said, frustrated.

"About?" Lucas replied.

"The people, the sky, or maybe how you struggle to hold a conversation, anything!"

"I wouldn't find it as hard if I had the time to talk, or if there was something worth talking about."

A week ago, Lucas sat staring out the window of his apartment. He had been silent as he ignored the sound blasting from the TV. Lucas could see the glare flashing in the reflection of the window, the news was on, but he did not want to know what it was trying to tell him.

Down the side of the building vertically, his eyes attempted to travel, then across the stream of car traffic and up the buildings across the street. There in the windows of the building opposite him other televisions glowed and flashed. The night had taken over the city so all sorts of moving, unnatural lights had become its life.

"The meals I cooked, the movies we watched, the interesting people we pass by when we drive through the rough part of town?"

"I was busy eating and being polite at the table when you cooked, I was shushed if I made a peep during a movie, which is the best time I find to talk about movies. And the people we pass by when we drive are all nuts. That is the end of the story."

"You didn't like my food?" Noah asked.

"I loved your food and where I grew up, silence was the sign of a good meal." Lucas bowed his head a little, blushing. There was silence in between the two of them.

Gunshots from the street broke the thick wall of quiet that neither of them could find a way to break through. Sirens, more gunshots, and finally an explosion that neither of them seemed too utterly shocked about came flooding up at them.

Noah raced down the hall, pounding on Lucas's door. Lucas stood up from the window sill and unlocked his door. There was no greeting needed.

Noah grabbed Lucas's arm and dragged him out of his apartment, Lucas locked his door fast, his keys hanging from his belt loop. Lucas was shuffled into Noah's apartment.

The TV was on in the living room with the same images as it was in Lucas's. The channel was different, Noah watched more serious conservative programs, while Lucas watched whichever news he clicked to first, he always figured it was the same general news just with a different spin.

"Another few bite the dust," Lucas laughed a little.

"How can you joke about that?" Noah asked.

"Now you don't want me to talk then?"

"No, please talk, oh silent one that seems to be happy with what could be the end of the world."

"Could be? It is. The end is here. It's been five days since the power went out, but I kind of wasted your batteries on your radio last night. Not even the people broadcasting on

70

the frequencies I listened to knew what day the sunlight would actually stop. So would you rather laugh at the chaos around us or become a part of it?" Lucas looked straight up into the sky.

"I guess laugh. What about our families though?"

"Mine disowned me when I came out. Dad gave me thirty minutes to pack my suit cases and get out, so my mind is pretty much just on watching the end of it all right now." Lucas picked up a few black roof pebbles and tossed them into the air.

"My parents might still be alive; I haven't talked to them since they joined up with that cult. The Eye,..." Lucas used his fingers to make it look like he had a third eye on his for head.

"Can we not talk about that? I don't think you ever mentioned your parents kicked you out though," Noah said cutting him off.

"Correction, my father kicked me out and my mother stood by and did nothing."

"I'm sorry."

"You had nothing to do with it. Can we be quiet and just let this be the seventh day, the day the sun goes out when it goes down?"

"Did they kick you out recently?"

"No. It was like ten years ago I was sixteen. You really like to talk, don't you?" Lucas asked.

"You've known me for three weeks, we have been together every other night until the newscast about the sun going out and how we wouldn't be effected until day seven. Then you slept over, I would think you know enough to know I love to talk," Noah said.

"I stayed so you'd have someone around to listen, plus who the fuck would want to be alone when the world ends?" Lucas leaned over to look down on the city streets more intensely.

71

"I don't agree with the news cast, I don't agree with the radio, and I am going to say it for the first time, I don't agree with you." Noah waved his hands wildly.

"About the end of the world?" Lucas scratched his head.

"I think we are going to wake up tomorrow, and the sun will rise, and the world will keep spinning, and the things we say now will still have value," Noah said, one of his hands playing with a single key in his pocket. The rest of his keys were lying in a bowl on his bookshelf right next to the door of his apartment.

"What is that in your pocket?" Lucas asked, avoiding the situation he could see coming a mile away.

"I got you a key made." Noah pulled it out and slipped it into Lucas's clutched fist.

"The world is over and you are giving me a key to your place?"

"Just take it and use it sometime." Noah crossed his arms and stepped back.

"That might be a hard task when your door is always unlocked."

"Then lock it for me."

"When did you have this made, Noah?"

"The Friday after we started hanging out."

"That's a little bit soon to have a key made for someone."

"Lucas, it's a little bit early to be brushing your teeth in someone else's apartment when you live down the hall."

"My water was brown."

"You left your toothbrush there." Noah avoided eye contact.

"The super never got around to fixing my sink."

"You think it doesn't matter, so it doesn't, move on." Noah backed off even more.

"The sink matters, my toothbrush matters, it all matters. If the sun comes up or not it all matters to me."

"Are you trying to tell me something?" Lucas walked over to Noah and gave him a funny look.

Two days had passed since the news had spoken for the first time of impending doom and Noah and Lucas had practically started living together. Lucas was an early riser, but that night, Noah could not get to sleep so he paced the floor in the kitchen, thinking over everything that came into his mind. At one point he had even openly started talking to god, even though he wasn't sure god was listening.

This is what woke Lucas up. Lucas stumbled down the hall and into the kitchen, where in the light, Noah looked like some kind of saint. Lucas stepped into the light and took Noah's hand, silently leading him back to bed.

Once they were both under the covers, Lucas was asleep again, but Noah lay awake. His eyes gazing at Lucas, if this was the end of the world, then Noah was alright with it. That was the last night they had power.

"Nahh, just if we didn't wake up... I like you a lot." Silence came back and so did the noises of chaos from all around them. They paced and leaned and watched as time ticked by slowly. The sun went from beating on their heads to the sides of their faces and finally below the skyline of the city. The darkness grew and the stars came out one by one.

"You wanna talk about what we want to wake up to?" Lucas smiled; they had laid down to look up at the moon.

"I want to wake up to..."

"Say it, god damn it..." Lucas laughed.

"You," Noah said not feeling the need to constantly talk. Then came the final silence, and tired eyes, and sleep.

***

(A Secret Note from Fynn)

I know that this note is not actually that secret. However, there is a wonderful reason I did not mention it in the Table of Contents. This, for those of you that have read all the way through this fantastic, might I even say "fynntastic" little collection of short stories. I have come a long way from putting out my first book, never the less from the first story I ever tried to write.

While we are right before the end, I would like to thank you. I would like to invite you to write your own stories, make your own books. It may be hard at first, but it is worth it. One day, you will wake in the middle of the night with the most bizarrely unique idea. This idea will haunt you until you have written it down.

(By the way if you are up in the middle of the night right now either cause I have you hooked, or that very idea is waiting… write it,… now!)

The story you are about to read is the one that started me off, not only on writing, but imagining, acting, dreaming, believing in things no one else might ever understand. I swore so many times never to let it out. It is my best homage to Sir J.M Barrie. I hope he is alright with that.

Anyway, back to you, the reader. Enjoy, dream, live, and most of all never let anyone stand in the way of your fantasies.

Yours Truly, Michael "Fynn" Lange

***

The Darling Diaries
~Michael~

~~~The House and Family Today~~~

"Time has changed a land once innocent. Years have made the ageless evil." The last sentence scribbled in a dusty diary. There were four different styles of hand writing all telling their own stories, but this last sentence seemed so, unworthy. Thousands of dear diary entries, just to be finished by one sentence, with nothing but pages screaming for stories of their own afterward. He could hear his grandmother climbing the stairs, closer and closer. He shoved the old diary back into the ancient chest he had found it in. He quickly grabbed the closest box and carried it out to the truck. Michael's grandmother, Lilly, had given up on living in the same house as her family had lived in for generations on end. The conversation why went something like this.

"It's about time I moved to the country. I am quite old after all," Lilly would say for the hundredth time.

"But, Mom, this house, it's been in the family for ages," Michael's mother would say pleading.

"So have I, if you want the house, fine. You take it, but my time here is long gone," Lilly would say. Here is where mother and daughter gave one another a look of complete misunderstanding.

"Mom, I just think you should stay here, you've never lived anywhere else. To be honest, moving at your age isn't a good idea."

"At my age, I should not be questioned. I am older, and therefore wiser. What I want is to be closer to my grandchild while I still can be." A look of guilt was sent from mother to daughter.

"Mom, please try not to talk like that, I'm sure you'll be here a lot longer, you are still young after all."

"I know I am very old, older than any women have ever been in our family. I have made up my mind, Sara. I am not living here any longer. I am done with this house and all its shadows." Then Lilly would comment on how the house only brought her heartache and regret and the conversation would end.

Michael took a box passed Grandmother Lilly, as she double checked the other rooms. The last thing out of her bedroom was a painting of her mother, Jane, her twin Moira and herself. Michael always thought they looked the same. Grandmother Lilly now looked like Jane, and his mother Sara now looked like Lilly. One by one all the boxes were moved out of the attic and driven to the country side. There was brief conversation on which boxes were going to which rooms in the country house. The box full of old toys and books would go into the guest room for when Michael was old enough to have children of his own. The tea sets would find a new home in a hutch in the dining room. And last, but definitely not least, the art supplies would get their own room with the biggest window and the most light. He got to the top of the stairs one last time and there Lilly was looking at the chest as if she was waiting for it to open up and talk.

"Do you want me to take this one, Grams?" he asked her, as he tried to move it.

"No, Michael, that chest stays here. It belongs to the house, and whatever lucky family gets it next." Lilly turned to him and shooed him out of the room.

This made his mind race. Why was this chest the only thing she was leaving behind? And how did it belong to the house?

Two days passed and the house was emptied, all except for Michael's sleeping bag and of course, the chest he could not stop thinking about. He went to roll up his sleeping bag with his mother waiting in the car, engine reeving. She stood in the doorway looking at him over her shoulder. The look in her eyes was one of seeing someone she had wanted to meet decades ago, but never had. He held his sleeping bag under his arm, with the keys to the house in his left hand, all ready to leave for once and for all. Lilly turned to face him, fully stopping him in his tracks.

"I am asking you for one night to protect this place," she said with a loving smile.

"Grams, there's really not much left to protect, beside that ancient chest in the attic."

"Then you will have an easy time with your task I am quite sure. I shall see you when your mother takes you home in the morning, Michael." She kissed his forehead. The kiss on his forehead felt different than others, she really was blessing him.

Michael waited at the door, waving as his mother and grandmother drove down the street. He closed the door then went to the window, watching them drive passed Kensington gardens.

Once his mother's car was out of sight, Michael ran up the stairs as fast as he could to the chest in the attic. He looked around at the empty room. This room was the old nursery, but had been used as an attic for thirty years at least.

He opened the black chest gently. He could tell it had been there for ages just waiting, probably since before his grandmother was born. He took out some of the items, placing them gently on the floor. An old book, a few wooden animals, an ancient teddy bear, and a small leafy green box. He had never had the time to look at these things, only recently had he even known the chest was there. He palmed the small box, and opened it. Inside was a silver acorn on a thin long silver necklace chain. He held it, not sure why, it seemed as if it was calling to him. He picked up the necklace, unhooking the chain in the back. He placed it around his own neck. It carried a bit more weight than he thought it should. Michael closed the leafy box and went to read more of the diary. He flipped through the pages and stopped to read.

~Dear Diary,

It is spring time once again and I have a feeling this might be the one. I finally have my chance to join the stars. I noticed from my perch at the nursery window that the last few nights, the sky has been suspiciously clear. I can see all the stars and I have tried to count them but I count differently each time so I am not sure where the real star lies. I am wondering if Grandmother has been lying to me, Mom never speaks of such fantasies. That is all I have to write for tonight.

~Moira

Page after page of Moira's entries spoke of the stars and the moonlit sky. Michael left the book open on the floor. He walked over to the window, curious about Moira's stars. The sky seemed eerily clear; his eyes scanned every single star. Moonlight caressed the buildings, backyards and foliage of Kensington Gardens. He carefully unlocked and opened the window. Without any effort the window swung right open, not even a single squeak. A gush of wind rushed in flipping the book's pages and closing the attic door. A smell rode the wind, crisp, cold sea air. Michael backed away from the window and back to the book. The page read:

~Dear Diary,

I know mother tells me the stars will take me soon, but since I have turned eighteen, I think I have missed my chance. Moira went years ago, or so she says. She has moved away now, in search of other adventures. We no longer talk. I have never seen the sky as clear as it is supposed to be. In short I have given up; I am locking the window since it is my last night in the nursery.

~Lilly

He flipped to the next page with his forefinger.

"Time has changed a land once innocent. Years have made the ageless evil."

His feet took him back to the open window; one star seemed to stand out almost as if it was closer than all the others. The lights in the house flickered and dimmed, then went out altogether. Michael made his way to the attic door; his hand twisted the knob behind his back. Moonlight seeped in through the open window filling the room dimly, as shadows seemed to dart back and forth, playing with Michael's mind. He was getting worried about what he had just gotten himself into, and just now started to think there might actually be something to keep safe in this house after all. He swore to himself that the shadows weren't moving, they weren't trying to crawl to the old black chest.

"After all, how could they be, this kind of thing just didn't happen outside of books," he thought.

Suddenly, a silhouette appeared in the window, a living shadow from a time long gone. It walked in a slow, long stride toward Michael and the chest.

"Go away, leave, back into the night," Michael said with the box now at his side. He reached down fast, pulling out an old rusted sword. "I'll stick this right through you, I am not afraid of shadows." He lunged toward the shadow.

"Shadows aren't what you should be afraid of," a voice came from nothingness.

The wind blew in from the window strong and fast knocking Michael into the old chest. He was soon joined by the diary and the other things as the shadows seemed to throw them in after him. The lid slammed shut trapping him in darkness. Quickly after the slam, a horrid scrapping noise surrounded him. Michael was being dragged across the floor. There was a sudden drop and nothing. But still the lid wouldn't budge as he kicked his legs as hard as he could. Soon his mind told him to give up, so he sat there for what seemed like forever.

81

****~~~A World Long Locked Up~~~****

Cold, isolated, desolate Michael awoke in darkness with the chest still surrounding him. Holding his fears tight beside him, he kicked and struggled, shaking the box in an effort to get out. Water splashed against the chest's sides. He kicked as hard as he could and the lid finally popped open. His feet met with icy grey water up to his knees. Taking the diary with him, he walked onto the dulled gray sand of the beach. Michael left the other things behind.

He looked at his new environment, only to find an island that looked like it would be better off if the sea just flowed over it. It was as if all the life had been sucked out the island a millennia ago. The trees that lined the beach stood dark and lifeless, each and every one had died in a slow, tortured way. The waves splashed at Michael's feet over and over as he looked out to the sea, nothing but water and sky. The horizon where water met air was a malicious purple, its clouds threatening of violent storms.

Michael walked further onto the shore until the dead black forest ate him whole. Little black clouds moved from tree to tree, as fast as fire. Michael walked deeper into the forest, hoping to find some little bit of salvation from this ancient place.

After an hour, he found another desolate gray shore. He noticed not too far off was a shipwreck. He had never seen one before, but he still knew this one was not common. Michael approached it to find the ship to be made out of stone, old vines climbing its sides. Surly, this ship could never float. How then did it still have barnacles clinging to it? He dared not venture aboard, as he was afraid of the man bold enough to make a ship of rock. Michael took full stride away from the ship only to find himself deep in the woods, countless screaming, and tortured trees around him. With every slight breeze, the sound of their agony heightened. He grew angry trying to find his way out of this desert of a jungle. Hour upon hour of the same trees clawing at his skin only led to a clearing.

A circle of midnight black trees surrounded the clearing. And there in the exact middle was a single tree older than all the rest, the only one that was still alive. Jealous green weeds all around it slowly crawling to it, wanting to suck every little drop of life out. The tree called out to Michael, beckoning him closer. He obeyed without a single thought, walking right up to the tree as if it were an old friend. Michael's head was slowly filling itself up with whispers, thousands of tiny voices with no true form. The clouds of soot were waiting behind the trees that circled him. They appeared, more and more of them, with each voice he heard the night like cloud they formed grew. He touched the tree. There was an explosion of whispers as the little floating spheres of soot grew nearer and nearer, surrounding him and the tree. Michael could understand little bits and pieces here and there.

"Thoughts of sorrow. Ageless evil. Seek the fairy that once was his."

He pressed himself against the tree, trying to stay away from these little balls of sadness. Michael felt the tree with his hands, grabbing for anything to defend himself, as they got closer, louder, and darker.

"Thoughts, of Sorrow…Ageless Evil…Seek the Fairy that once was His." He grabbed at a knot in the tree's trunk, "Thoughts, of sorrow," the voices grew louder, he twisted the knot in his hand.

"Ageless evil." Michael grew nervous of what these little things wanted with him so he closed his eyes tight.

"Seek the fairy." Finally after about four fast twists of the knot, the ground opened up beneath his feet.

"That once was hissssssss!" Once again he fell into darkness.

****~~~The Underground~~~****

When Michael opened his eyes, he found himself in a torch lit cavern. The flickering of the flames bounced shadows across the dirt walls. He could see where the tree above had come from. In the middle of the room was a cage-like structure where most of the tree roots met, with a nest built in the center. Cobwebs hung from the ceilings and small brown mushrooms sprouted from the floor. A few shelves and baskets hung around, holding a strange array of items.

There was a shuffling from up above, something moving about above ground, trying to get down. Michael looked for ways whatever it was up there could get down. The hole he had fallen through closed up right after it had taken him. He felt the walls for another way out, since he really didn't want to find out what was above him. Michael felt every inch of dirt wall and root, just hoping one would lead him into another cavern or tunnel and not up. He found nothing on the walls or floor, so he climbed into the nest. Once his full weight was on the nest, it flipped, plunging him into an underground river. The river carried Michael through bright blue caves. The walls of the underground river shifted colors as the stalactites and stalagmites looked more and more like ferocious crocodiles. His heart beat like a clock, echoing off the stone around him.

Finally, he was rushed back into the light as the river's flow deposited him in a large shallow bay.

~~~Hot on the trail~~~

Michael sloshed his way to the closest beach. This one was covered black with cooled lava, and vents that pumped steam out into the still air. Boiling pools of red magma spit searing juice straight up with hot mist. He could see the mountain that had caused all this with its top blown off, as well as the border of dead trees where lava hadn't reached. This landscape seemed to shine as much as it bled.

Michael stared in amazement as he noticed diamonds littered the ground. Then he noticed yet another oddity, there were foot prints also embedded into the solid waves of lava. He followed the footsteps. They led him all over the black, hard ground as if there had once been a maze but the walls had faded away. Finally after a long walk, looking down for his next step he looked up to find a young woman, frozen in diamond. Michael examined every inch of her diamond skin, trying to find some clue about who she was. With nothing else to turn to, he opened the diary and searched. His diary spoke of Indians in some passages, pirates in others, mermaids, nymphs and other creatures. He read a description of the Indian Princess. It was a match. He looked within her palm. She had been holding something. A broach of some sort. It looked familiar, almost exactly like the one his Great Aunt Moira had been wearing in the family painting.

"Poor girl," he thought to himself and walked away, leaving her alone once again.

~~~A Dark Dance~~~

As he got closer to the forest's edge, he could see the darkness within, the little balls of soot shot around. His ears could hear sharp cords of music, which made the hair on the back of his neck stand up. He looked back and the diamond Indian princess was pointing him in the direction he had chosen.

His feet found the beat of a native drum, with the crunch and snaps of the twigs at his feet. Michael seemed to pick up a dance once immersed in the woods and the cloud creatures were his audience. It was slow, tedious, and draining, but he resisted the urge to run from it. It guided him, helping him further and further into the woods. Michael closed his eyes as words formed deep in his mind.

"Drum, drum.... drum, drum.... Destroyed is joy. Gone is light, and rising is the nightmare. Drum, drum... drum, drum..." the words repeated, stronger and repeated again as his body swayed through the dead brush.

"Drum, drum... Find boys of old, in caves of shadows past yet not quite forgotten. Drum drum..." The first part was sung again and it took on a cycle. Then a new line was added, the words made Michael's eyes shoot open as they screamed in his head over and over, "Kill the darkness that is killing us." He started running to the beat, his body out of his control.

~~~Traded~~~

These clouds of soot gave him yet another trail to follow, another path with no other options. He found himself again back at the stone ship, running straight toward it, as he had been going in a giant circle. Each mental whisper, no matter which voice it came from, urged him to move toward the stone ship. As much as he feared its hard cold presence, he wanted to get these things off of his back. He scaled its side, dashed through a stone arch way, and stumbled down a staircase into a dimly lit chamber. There was a creature, not quite human, but not like anything Michael had ever seen before. The creature faced away from him. It was almost as tall as he was, he saw its legs. Its spiny back draped in clothes made of leaf and vine. The being's hands on an ancient piano, its long brown hair hung past its hips. A few notes played from the old piano as its gentle, odd fingers hit the keys. Light from above hit its hands to finally show their true color, it turned to him. Her midnight purple face, her empty brown eyes, her skinny dark form, darker than the spheres that had guided him here. She was like that color of the night sky with a new moon, yet you could still see every little freckle and scar.

"Hello, boy." Her voice seemed to be accompanied by a chime of bells.

"Hello," he was stunned by her unique beauty.

"By that look on your face, I can tell you have plenty of questions to ask me."

"Do I look that lost?" he asked. She shook her head "I don't know where I am, or even why I'm here?" he said.

"You're a Darling, I can tell by those eyes. You should know the name of this place; it's in your blood… it's part of your family's history."

"You are home. All of the Darlingbirds have a home in the Neverland," she said as his face filled with utter disbelief. "Don't believe me. I would not either, not after so much

87

change. This place used to be pure imagination, now I think it is more of a nightmare, as do most people."

"What do you mean? How does a place just simply change? I thought this is where all the happy thoughts and day dreams went."

"It was, a long time ago, before he couldn't leave. When the fairies first had me bring him here, he had such a strong imagination that the island just became a part of him. He is so strong when it comes to emotion. Then something changed, I think it had a lot to do with your world, it was leaking in. Making the Neverland go from summer to fall. That day he couldn't leave was when it finally lost the ability to go back."

"Please, tell me what happened here, what it used to be like." Michael sat down across from her.

"It used to be a lush jungle, clear warm blue water, and there were beasts that could never be found anywhere else. Now sadly, I don't think they will ever be found again. One day, somewhere around spring cleaning ages ago, he tried to leave. He never made it past the horizon. It seemed he was locked here, as much as he believed he just couldn't escape. So he grew sad, which in turn made his shadow grow. Did you know that's where all your sorrow goes? Into your shadow?"

"No, I didn't. What did that have to do with this island, though?"

"Well, when he grew sad, the water turned icy and grey, the trees started to die one by one. I went to try and save it all, but I failed horribly. I went to the Fairy King to make a wish so I could be his happy thought. It made him worse; he hated me for trying to replace the Darlings." Michael's jaw dropped.

"He grew angry, furious in fact, then the volcano blew, fires destroyed the native camps, lava took down the maze and the entire fairy kingdom. I blame myself for half of what's gone on around here. The fairies blame me for all of it. They punished me to be the darkest glow of all so that he would never love me. They are still furious with me, which is why they have become the little spheres of soot, that I am sure you've seen."

"Yeah, they kind of took me here; I just couldn't stand their voices in my head anymore."

"You're lucky they talk to you. In fact, I am surprised you understand their language. Maybe it's that Darling in you. They have been ignoring me, along with the children from your world, for years now. They only have one emotion left. It used to be a fairy can only have one emotion at a time. There used to be such a wide range, now it's just anger."

"They kept asking me to find the fairy that once was his. Are you the one they were talking about?" She looked at him with a blank expression.

"You can save us," she said after a long pause.

"How can I save you?" he asked, totally out of it.

"I'll get their attention. I will distract them long enough for you to run. I will draw you a map and show you where to go, he will be there. Find him, save him. Save the Neverland." She moved around franticly. She took the journal from him, drawing out a map on a blank page.

"Ok. I'll do it."

They planned it out. The midnight fairy flew out into the open, her skin glowed brighter than any other light Michael had ever seen. He could not stay to watch her, however. She soared above the ship. All the little angry black soot clouds converged upon her. She hovered out by the crow's nest, light breaking and cracking through her midnight skin. The little black clouds jetted toward her, as if to stop this light from escaping. Michael ran out over the side of the ship and rushed, looking over his shoulder as her now white pure fairy form was engulfed by darkness. An explosion of light and the noise of bells emerged, stunning the dark fairies. Michael fell from the force of it, he quickly got right back up, running as fast as his legs would let him.

She was gone, Michael thought her name in his head. He had heard about her and now he believed in her as hard as he could. As much as he knew she had traded her life to save this place. Michael hoped, as he ran through the dense wood, that he would not make her death a waste.

~~~From Boy to Bird~~~

He went full stride as fast as he could away from the ship, into the dead forest, hoping to find this spot the fairy had showed him. Each tree seemed to move out of his way, giving him space so he could get to his destination as fast as possible. Behind him grew impassable thorn bushes to stop the onslaught of fairies trying to end a light that now seemed to be a part of him. He felt lighter on his feet now, almost as if his feet weren't even touching the ground. He could hear the voices again. They were getting closer making his head throb.

"Snuff, extinguish, kill," is all he could hear now circling him.

Michael stopped as the woods became pitch black around him, there was no escape. They would extinguish his light as easy as one would blow out a candle. Suddenly he felt a surge inside of himself. His skin was radiating a pure gold. They rushed at him now, and he shot straight up into the air, his body jetting out of the tree tops. The fairies collided in the space he left behind. He floated there for a second, unsure of what was going on, then it hit him, he was flying. Michael smiled and took off as fast as he could to find the shadow boy.

~~~Too Long In-betwixt and In-between~~~

Michael could see the entire island from this height. He opened the dairy and looked at the midnight fairy's sketch of the island. She had placed an X on the ocean, he thought it might be a mistake, but trusting her, he flew the way he was directed. There on the horizon, in the middle of the water, rose a collection of boulders that looked eerily like the remains of a destroyed castle and a skull all at once. As he got closer, he could see skeletons lining where the waves and stone met. Some creatures did still inhabit this part of the water and as soon as he saw them, they saw him. The creatures plunged into the water, head over tail. From what he could tell, they were bony, copper skinned creatures with long seaweed green tails. He didn't want to think about a water landing, being that the only things he had seen here so far, besides the midnight fairy, had meant some kind of harm to him. He landed softly on the rock high above the water, possibly an old balcony that resembled one of the eyes of a skull. The glow from his skin faded as soon as the cold sea air hit his back, making him walk deeper into the eye of the skull castle. Out of the wall walked the shadow boy himself. The shadow was his size and shape, in fact it could have been him if it weren't purely shadow. Michael backed up from it, to no avail, he found himself on the edge of the rock. About to fall backward into the sea, Michael spoke in an effort to not join the bony sea creatures.

"Who are you?" he called to it.

It stopped its advance.

"I am youth, I am sorrow," the shadow said.

Michael was stunned, he had heard his own voice for the first time.

"I was sent here by a fairy with midnight skin."

"Why didn't she come with you?" The shadow boy was clearly untrusting of anyone.

"The fairies got her, I'm sorry." Michael took out the diary.

"Are you the one that all these girls were writing about?" He handed the shadow the book, but the shadow could not hold onto it, and the book fell right through his black hands.

"I can't touch it. If I could, I wouldn't be able to read it anyway. You read it, or I'll push you off into the sea with the merthings." It pulled a black dagger from its side.

"Ok, ok. Calm down, I'll read it." Michael flipped through the pages and read a few entries about the fabulous adventures of Darlingbirds and a boy named Pan. One about the time they defeated a hooked villain disguised as a ringmaster, another describing their adventures with the Indian princess, the last one about how the boy saved the entire fairy kingdom by playing his panpipe. The last entry he read was one of the first, about how the boy saved the first Darlingbird, her brothers, as well as his own gang from a hooked villain and an entire ship full of pirates on his own.

"That's enough, stop. How did you get your hands on such a book?" it asked, holding its dagger to Michael's bare throat.

"It was in an old chest in the attic, I think my grandmother was the last one to write in it."

"And which bird was she?" It withdrew its dagger.

"That's the thing; I don't think she was one. I don't think you ever showed up for her, so she closed the window, and locked it. The last thing in here is what happened when you didn't show up."

"I don't need to hear that. I know what happened, she locked the window and trapped me here."

"I don't think she meant to, she just didn't believe. In fact, I didn't believe in the stories either, until I ended up here."

It started floating as if to take off deep into the skull.

"Wait, I think I can help you." Michael stepped closer to it, it took off and he chased it. Tunnel after tunnel twisting and turning here and there, so far he had no clue which way he had come. Then suddenly, at the end of the next cave was a door. Michael figured the shadow must have gone right through it. He pushed it open into a room with no ceiling, high stone walls and the cold grey sky up above. A small pool of water waited in the center of the floor. The shadow was floating above the pool, its arms crossed, one leg bent the other hanging straight down.

"I don't need your help," it stated in a monotone voice.

"She sent me to help you. Does that mean anything? My grandmother Lilly left me in the house to protect your chest. Does that mean anything?"

The shadow grunted. "There's only one thing to be done."

"If it gets me home, I'll do it."

"I was given everlasting youth in trade for my love."

"Love, you can trade that?"

"With fairies, yes. For a long time, I enjoyed it, but the second I talked to the Wendybird, I wanted to have it back."

"You would have aged for her?"

"She has my love, and she always will. I gave it to her to keep her safe."

"I'm sorry, but she's passed away years ago."

"I know that." It uncrossed its arms then crossed them again.

"Without my love, I can never leave. I can never grow old. Age seemed to please her so. I am guessing it will make me happy too."

"That means one day you will pass."

"I know. I need you to find me my love, it was somewhere in that chest. Go back to it, search it, and find me my love."

"How do I get back there, though? I don't think those creatures are going to let me go by water."

"Simply need to get there and you will find a way," the shadow said fading into the walls behind him.

Michael looked up at the gray sky wondering if he could fly again, now that the shadow was gone.

~~~Just Think~~~

"Simply need," Michael thought to himself.

"Guess that's the same as think happy thoughts." He sat on the cold stone floor and concentrated, trying to focus on what he needed.

~~~Clouds of ash, became fields of beauty~~~

His needing thoughts led Michael's mind back to the beach, only to see the empty box, all its contents gone. Then his mind wandered farther to places in the Neverland that no one had ever ventured to. With his mind fixated his body soon followed and like a bolt of lightning he was off.

Over the choppy water, the shore, trees and to the charred remains of the natives' camp and fort. He landed, walking beyond the desecrated camp. Michael stumbled upon a field filled with strangely vibrant flowers. Each and every one seemed to have a different color and bud; no two would ever be the same. Michael took his first step. Where crushed flowers should have been there was a ghost like mist. It was as if the flowers that should be beneath his foot had never existed. He kept walking. Whenever he lifted his foot, the mist took shape of the strangely vibrant flowers once again. He moved further into the field, hesitant of the magic that kept the buds of mist alive. He noticed the mist more and more with each step, he saw his questions coming to life as if to taunt him. With every step he could see his words wisp around his feet, they were white and thin.

"What is this place?"

"I am alone, why do I feel like someone's watching me struggle?"

"Is this my quest or was it meant for someone else?" Then the ghostly mists would lead into his next step, another wisp, and twice as many questions stung his mind, slowing his pace.

Out of his view, the words like snakes slithered upon each other, all building up into a being that's feet no longer touched the ground. A spirit, a ghost, purely made of white mist. The heavy white words formed its boots, pants, long captain's coat, its wicked face with ice cold blue eyes, the long greasy hair that seemed to be the darkest words, and finally on the end of its right arm, was a sharp, steel hook. Even made out of mist, you could see the glimmer of the blade just waiting to claw into flesh, craving to take away unending youth. The ghost made its way toward Michael, who was getting weaker and weaker with every step he took.

Michael turned out of instinct. He froze at the sight of this man, who was clearly not dead, but no longer alive either. The spirit got close enough for Michael to see every little detail in his smooth face, and most of all, those piercing baby blue eyes. Pain suddenly filled the side of Michael's chest. He looked down at where the spirit's right hand should have been, what he saw was the ending of that sharp, deadly, sinister steel hook. He could feel the hook buried deep in his side, cold as ice. His clothing started to deepen in color, there was a red emerging where there shouldn't be. He knew there was no hook, no blood, but the world around him was fading as he fell to his knees, gripping his side. Finally, Michael fell face down into the mist.

~~Once~~

He awoke with a warm feeling on his chest. He
grasped at it, no blood, no slice, just the necklace he had put
on before this had all started. He felt the silver acorn with his
hand, it was warm and soothing. Michael looked around, the
flowers were all gone and the island seemed to be alive again.
He could smell a fire nearby and the scent of spring all around
him. His skin color seemed dull compared to the vibrant blue
skies, the luscious green grass; the essence of the island was
totally different. He moved, swiftly floating just off of the
ground.

Out of the woods ahead of him, came a line of five
boys all under the age of ten, skipping and frolicking. They
seemed to pay no attention to Michael, as if he wasn't there at
all. Out of the brush, a girl with long blonde hair and a red
headed boy. He knew who they were from the second he saw
them. He knew every adventure they had ever been on and
how all of this would end. Michael followed them around,
watching them play out their little games with the Fairies,
Indians, and Pirates. Soon it was night time. All the boys had
gone off to bed, but the red headed one. The red headed boy
took the blonde girl's hand and guided her out of the home
underground. Together they flew to the old fairy kingdom.
The fairy kingdom was an old, majestic weeping willow. The
tree glowed with a golden light that was warm and pleasing as
a summer breeze. The boy took the girl's hand and they
started to glide into the sky slowly, dancing as if at a ball. She
held him close, her head on one shoulder, and her hand on the
other. He smiled, a brilliantly cocky smile, one hand in hers
the other on her hip. The fairies floated around them, dancing
slowly as well. Double moons softly lit their faces. The boy
stopped, he held both her hands.

"Wendy?" he asked curiously.

"Yes, Peter?"

"I have something for you, but you can't tell anyone,
alright?"

97

"Of course, I won't tell a soul." She smiled.

He pulled an acorn out his pocket, closed it in his palm tight, and concentrated.

When he opened his palm, there it was; the silver acorn. She put it on her necklace chain.

"Thank you, Peter. It's beautiful."

The world around Michael faded; he had seen all he needed to see. He was floating in the middle of the lava field, no trees around, the double moons cracking and crumbling overhead. He knew where Peter's love had gone. He jetted through the sky to the shadow's lair, landing gently.

"I've got it," he yelled "I found it."

There was no response. Michael started to wander through the caves for the shadow boy. A chill took him over, a light mist coated his feet. He stared into the darkness ahead.

"Hello," he said.

"Hello," echoed.

"I found what you asked me to …"

"I found…." echoed.

There in the mist was a young girl with long blonde hair; next to her was the red headed boy. Michael wasn't sure what to think, it could just be the hooked man, or it might really be Wendy, now back with her true love.

Michael stepped backward, finding his back against the wall, no place to go. He wasn't scared, just a little worried he might be handing the acorn over to the wrong spirit. Deep inside him, he wanted to keep the acorn to himself. The girl put out her hand palm up.

"May I have my kiss back, please?" Her voice filled with innocence.

Michael watched her as she seemed to solidify in front of him. He could see her skin color and the blue of her eyes. Michael's hand flew up to his chest, holding the acorn tight against his quickly beating heart.

"No, it's not yours," he stated, stepping away from the wall and the girl back-tracked. "This however…" He took out the book and threw it at her. It landed open, the pages flipping back and forth as if searching for an entry. The girl and boy disappeared in a puff of smoke.

Michael took off for the cave's entrance, jumping off the cliff. His feet left the hard rock and his body plummeted down into the cold, icy water. Legs kicking as fast as they could, striving to make it ashore, but failing. His body clung to a rock, halfway between the skull castle and the island. Michael was exhausted, he looked at where he had come from. The skull glared down, showing no signs of pity. The island seemed to tease him, looking across the waves. A breeze pricked at his wet skin as the waves rose around him. He was going to drown on this small rock. A skeleton hand was chained there by a dark red spot. Michael clearly wouldn't be the first one to die here.

The sea rose around him. A bird came bobbing along on its nest, first it went past him, content and fine with its situation.

"I'm dry and you're not," the bird seemed to be thinking as it floated around him.

Michael watched it get closer, its circles closing in on him. Finally its nest hit the rock; Michael was now only able to keep his arms and head out of the water. The bird looked at him. He looked back and they shared something that showed Michael a goodness he hadn't seen before. In that second, he decided that this bird was the only one to be trusted with his necklace. With one hand he took the necklace off and placed the necklace around the bizarre bird's neck. As it floated next to him the bird acknowledged the gift, bowing its head. It shook its long, off white wings and flew crowing a vibrant colorful noise that filled Michael's body. Suddenly he was warm again. The island in the distance slowly woke up, remembering its old self. The bird's crow helped the island to return to its lushness. Inch by inch the island creaked and moaned, stretching from its long sleep. Michael climbed into the now empty nest, floating away from the island.

When it seemed as if the island was sinking into the horizon, he could see a silhouette in the sky, a boy who would never grow up. Michael fell asleep in the nest, an arm hanging out here, a leg hung over there but never the less, he fell asleep.

~~~The Diaries~~~

When Michael awoke it was early morning and he found himself quite confused. His body had somehow ended up on a dock back in London. The seagulls cawing away at him, one in particular was quite miffed that Michael's head was in his nest, resting on the remnants of her eggs. He stood up, stretched, wiped some of the yolk from his hair, and headed back to the house. When he arrived back at his grandmother's house, he found his grandmother in the attic, looking out the window.

"So the stars took you?" she said.

"The shadows,..." He looked at her.

"I see. Well, I guess it's all over now, isn't it?"

"No. I think there's going to be more, just give it some time," Michael said, smiling at his grandmother.

That's the only talk about the island and its inhabitants that went on for many years. One day he would tell this to his children, and to make sure they could tell not only his story, but the ones of his elders, he wrote them all down, with plenty of blank pages to add on.

***

The End.

Made in the USA
Las Vegas, NV
13 June 2021

24634884R00056